Born

Story by
John Sobol

Pictures by
Cindy Derby

Groundwood Books
House of Anansi Press
Toronto   Berkeley

FLOATING COZILY in her mother's womb,
a baby waits to be born.

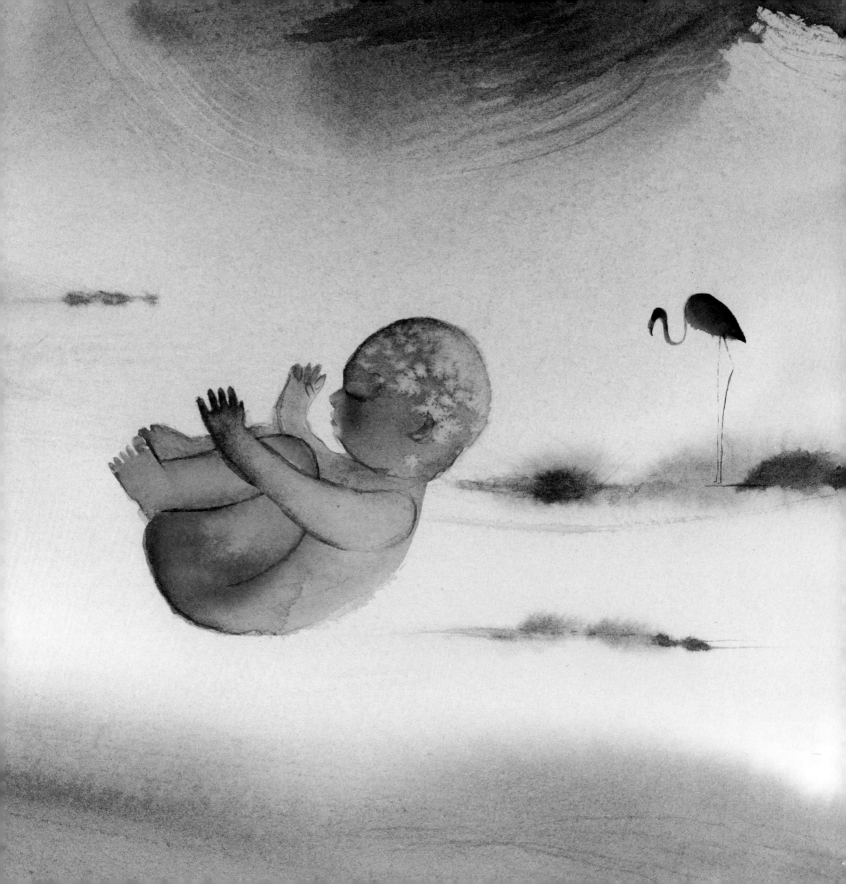

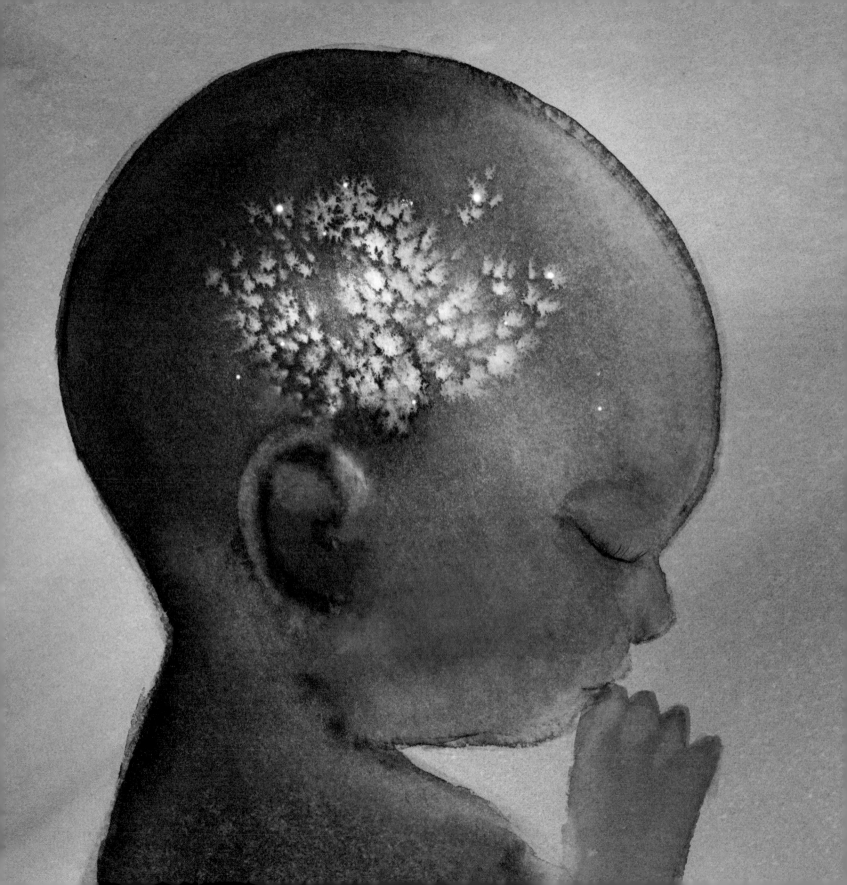

She has been floating — and
waiting — a long time. But she
doesn't mind. She likes it where she is.
The thump-thump of her mother's
heartbeat keeps her company, always.

She kicks out her foot and touches the edge of her world. Pushing against it is fun, so she kicks some more.

Soon she hears the
sweetest sound she knows.
A sound filled with love.
A song that surrounds her
and caresses her.

Hearing it, she relaxes,
and before long the song
carries her away to sleep.

Other times she is restless. Her legs
need to run, her arms need to hug,
her hands need to hold. More and
more she feels she is ready, but she
doesn't know for what.

Mostly, she feels a deep calm, safe at
home in the only home she has ever known.
Inside this beautiful world she is a vast
universe, and a small sprouting seed.

Now, something is happening.
Something different.

Her world is changing.
Strong currents lift her up
and away. Maybe *this* is what
she has been waiting for.

She squeezes
into a little ball,
tingling with
excitement.

Until suddenly there are new noises
and new feelings.
    She kicks out her foot but touches
nothing at all.
    She isn't floating anymore.
    Everything is different.

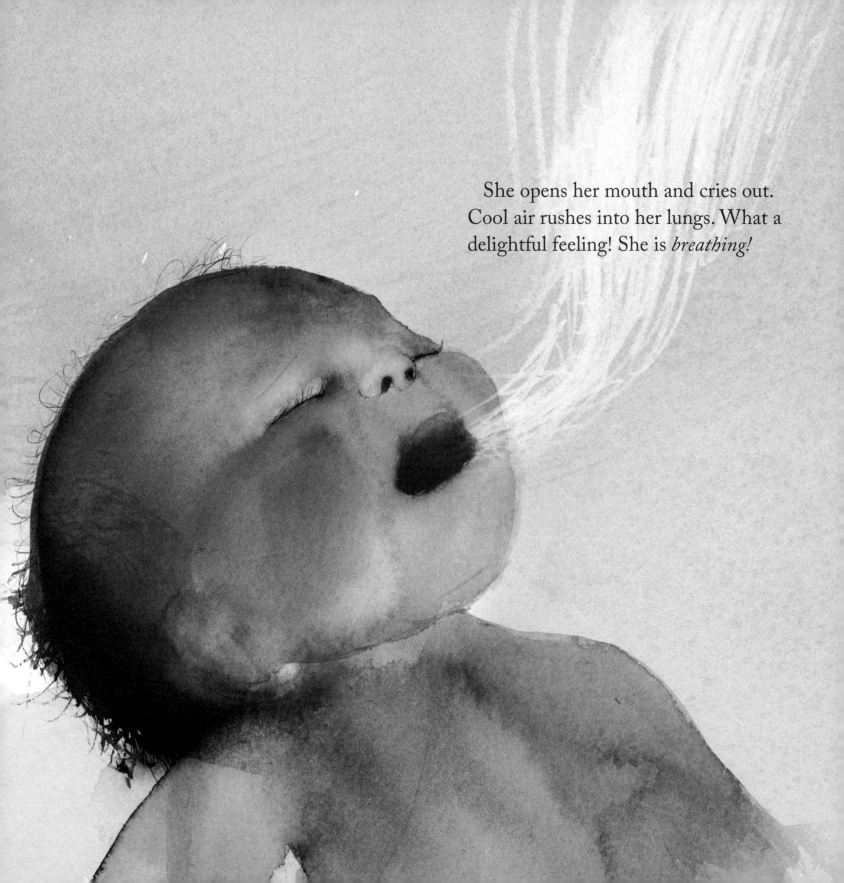

She opens her mouth and cries out. Cool air rushes into her lungs. What a delightful feeling! She is *breathing!*

Warm hands wrap her in scruffy softness.
    She feels herself lifted up and gently set
down.
    Where is she?

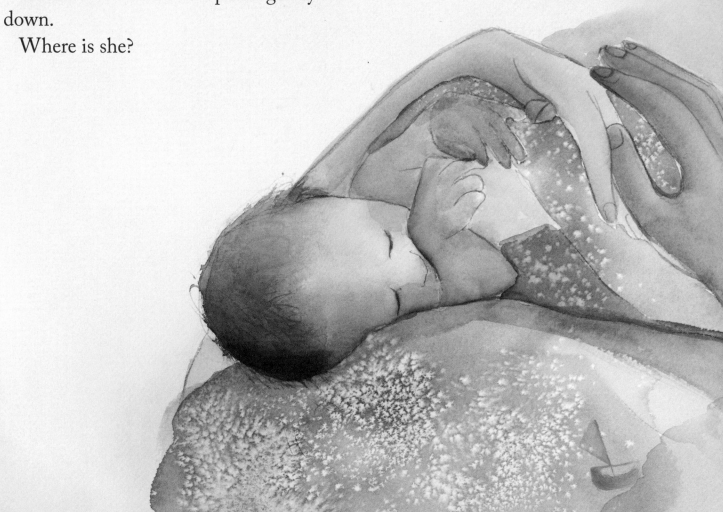

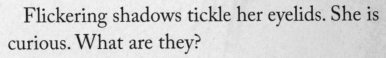

Flickering shadows tickle her eyelids. She is curious. What are they?

She opens her small uncertain eyes.

All she can see are fuzzy shapes and shifting shadows.

Until, whispering in her tiny ears, she hears the sound she loves most of all.

"Hello, sweetheart!"

She looks up at the sound, up into
her mother's eyes, filled with love.

Hearing her again, touching her again,
seeing her for the first time, she knows
she is where she needs to be. She smiles
a tiny smile.

And for the first time, the first of *many*
times, her mother looks deep into her eyes
and smiles back.

For she is *born*.

For every mother, and every child.
In joyful memory of Sheila Barry,
publisher and friend. — JS

For my mother. — CD

Groundwood Books / House of Anansi Press
groundwoodbooks.com

We gratefully acknowledge for their financial support of our
publishing program the Canada Council for the Arts, the Ontario
Arts Council and the Government of Canada.

Canada Council   Conseil des Arts
for the Arts   du Canada

ONTARIO ARTS COUNCIL
CONSEIL DES ARTS DE L'ONTARIO
an Ontario government agency
un organisme du gouvernement de l'Ontario

With the participation of the Government of Canada
Avec la participation du gouvernement du Canada | Canadä

Library and Archives Canada Cataloguing in Publication

Title: Born / story by John Sobol ; pictures by Cindy Derby.
Names: Sobol, John, author. | Derby, Cindy, illustrator.
Identifiers: Canadiana (print) 20190152338 | Canadiana
(ebook) 20190152370 | ISBN 9781773061696 (hardcover) |
ISBN 9781773064161 (EPUB) | ISBN 9781773064178 (Kindle)
Classification: LCC PS8637.O26 B67 2020 | DDC jC813/.6—dc23

The art was created in watercolor and digital collage.
Design by Michael Solomon
Printed and bound in Malaysia